HOWWWLLLL

MIXED UP

Bob Raczka

ILLUSTRATIONS BY
Chad Cameron

CAROLRHODA BOOKS MINNEAPOLIS

Carolrhoda Books
A division of Lerner Publishing Group, Inc.
241 First Avenue North
Minneapolis, MN 55401 U.S.A.

Website address: www.lernerbooks.com

Library of Congress Cataloging-in-Publication Data

Raczka, Bob.
   Fall mixed up / by Bob Raczka ; illustrated by Chad Cameron.
      p.   cm.
   Summary: The delights of autumn are described in mixed-up verse and
illustrations, and the reader is challenged to uncover the errors.
   ISBN: 978-0-7613-4606-7 (lib. bdg. : alk. paper)
   [1. Stories in rhyme. 2. Autumn—Fiction. 3. Humorous stories.]
I. Cameron, Chad, ill. II. Title.
PZ8.3.R1155Fal 2011
[E]—dc22   2009038922

Manufactured in the United States of America
1 - DP - 7/15/11

Dedicated to:

EVERY
BOY AND GIRL
WHOSE FAVORITE
SEASON IS FALL.

– B.R.

FoR Heather
-cc

Every Septober,
Every Octember,
Fall fills my senses with
scenes to remember.

Apples turn orange.
Pumpkins turn red.
Leaves float up into
blue skies overhead.

Bears gather nuts.
Geese hibernate.

Squirrels fly south in
big figure eights.

Scarecrows stand guard over candy corn sprouts. Milkweed pods open, and monarchs fly out.

Touchdowns are hit.
Home runs are kicked.

Kids leap in great
heaping piles of sticks.

Hats cover hands.
Gloves cover ears.
Bonfires cool off our
fronts and our rears.

Warm apple syrup,
Baked maple seeds,
And caramel pumpkins taste
yummy indeed.

Wolves say "Meow."
Black cats say "Whoo."
Horned owls howl at the full moon—
"How-OOOO!"

Mummies go bats.

Vampires ride brooms.

Tightly wrapped witches escape
from their tombs.

Neighbors give stuffing and drumsticks for treats.

Families give thanks
for a bounty of sweets.

Can this be fall?
Close, but not quite.
Go back and find all the
things that aren't right.